HONORED

HONORED

Roberta Kells Dorr

Fleming H. Revell
A Division of Baker Book House Co
Grand Rapids, Michigan 49516

© 2003 by Roberta Kells Dorr

Published by Fleming H. Revell
a division of Baker Book House Company
P.O. Box 6287, Grand Rapids, MI 49516-6287
www.bakerbooks.com

Printed in the United States of America

Library of Congress Cataloging-in-Publication Data
Dorr, Roberta Kells.
    Honored / Roberta Kells Dorr.
        p.   cm.
    ISBN 0-8007-1817-8
    1. Mary, Blessed Virgin, Saint—Fiction. 2. Bible N.T.—History of Biblical events—Fiction. 3. Christian women saints—Fiction. 4. Mothers and sons—Fiction. 5. Jesus Christ—Fiction. 6. Palestine—Fiction. I. Title.
PS3554.O694H66 2003
813′.54—dc21   2002154757

Scripture is taken from the King James Version of the Bible.

For my husband,
Dr. David C. Dorr, S.A.C.S.,
who like Luke was a physician.
He believed strongly enough
in the good news of the gospel
to give seventeen years of his life
to medical missions in the Middle East.

Many daughters have done virtuously, but thou excellest them all. Favour is deceitful, and beauty is vain; but a woman that feareth the LORD, she shall be praised.

Proverbs 31:29–30

stood on the deck of the small sailing vessel and looked down at my dear friend Theophilus on the dock. He had warned me against making this trip. "Those people are unfriendly," he'd said. "We're Greeks—they don't like us. Here, you're a physician with a popular clinic helping many people. What possible good can you do there?"

He knew that for a long time I had been eager to catch every bit of news from Jerusalem that told of a healer and prophet whose name was Jesus. Theophilus had scoffed at the very idea that these stories might be true.

"They're just fables told by poor peasants," he'd said. "Who would take seriously a story of angels appearing or a virgin giving birth? And didn't you tell me you'd heard about miraculous healings and even water turned to wine at a wedding?"

Before I knew it I had challenged him by insisting that I would travel to Jerusalem to discover the truth. Many of the people who had known this man, Jesus, were still alive, and I was determined to make every effort to find them. Theophilus was appalled that I had taken all of this so seriously.

As the ship pulled away from the dock and the figure of Theophilus grew smaller and smaller, I began to have second thoughts about my quest. What if I found it was all an invented story? What if I was viewed as an intruder with no right to be asking questions? I wanted, above all else, to see the mother of Jesus. I wanted to ask her about the angels and the strange story that she was still a virgin when she conceived this child. I, a physician, couldn't imagine such a thing.

The ship stopped at a port on the island of Cyprus and then sailed on down the coast of Palestine until it came to the port of Joppa. Here, to my surprise, two young men were waiting for me. One was dressed quite casually in a robe tied at the waist with a piece of hemp and sandals made of coarse leather. He had a thick beard and wore a head cloth wrapped carelessly around his head. He came forward, saying, "You must be Luke."

The other man was younger and had a friendly, almost shy demeanor. "I'm John," he said, "and this is Peter."

I didn't know what to say. They spoke rather clumsy Greek. I felt uncomfortable and even a bit foolish. They obviously were not scholars. Theophilus would have enjoyed the scene. He would have pointed out that I, an educated, sophisticated Greek, couldn't possibly have much in common with these men. I did have a moment of indecision when I even contemplated getting right back on the ship and returning to Antioch and my familiar world. But just then John pointed out that the ship had hoisted its sails and was moving away from shore.

"Come," Peter said, "we'll spend the night with my friend Simon the tanner, and then tomorrow we'll go to Jerusalem."

I immediately forgot about the ship and remembered why I had come. "Will the mother of your master see me?"

"Of course," John answered. "She is pleased that someone wants to hear her story. There have been many who want to know about her son, but they don't think to ask her."

So I went with them to the house of this tanner of Joppa. I remember little of the conversation or the food I was served, since I was preoccupied with the questions I would ask this woman who was the mother of the man known, even in Antioch, as Jesus of Nazareth.

Two days later John took me to the house of Jesus' mother, Mary, in Jerusalem. It was near the pool of Bethesda on the north side of the temple area. He knocked at an ancient door set in a stone wall that opened into a courtyard. It was some minutes before the door was opened by a young serving maid. She smiled shyly as John told her, "The Greek physician is here to speak with your mistress."

She motioned for us to come in, and John led me over to a couch beneath a massive grape arbor. I sat down on one of the mats and leaned on the armrest as I studied the pleasant, rather homey courtyard. There were banks of flowers growing in wild abandon in one large plot beneath an ancient almond tree. Near the couch was a smaller plot of herbs that gave off a fresh, even invigorating, fragrance. From somewhere beyond the open door that led into the living quarters, there came the sound of singing.

John motioned for me to stay where I was and then hurried through the door toward the source of the singing. I was surprised that the song was a rather simple, playful tune one would sing to a child. Abruptly the singing stopped, and a moment later a woman appeared at the door, carrying a birdcage with a small songbird inside.

"You must be Luke, the Greek physician," the woman said, smiling as she set down the birdcage and grasped one of my hands in her two outstretched hands.

"And you must be the mother of the man I have come to admire so much."

"Yes, I have the honor of being his mother," she said.

I noticed that she hadn't said, "I had the honor," as most would have said, but, "I have the honor," as though she were still his mother.

She motioned for me to sit down again and then reached for a large cushion and sat down across from me. As she adjusted her blue mantle, I noticed that her dark hair had streaks of gray. She was not young, but neither did she seem old. There were smile lines around her eyes and a gentleness about her that made me feel comfortable in her presence. And for just a moment a look of infinite patience—or perhaps sorrow—crossed her lovely face.

"You have come a long way," she said. "I think they said from Antioch."

I nodded, and for a moment I was so caught up in the excitement of actually sitting across from her that I couldn't think of anything to say. I was terribly frustrated. I had come so far with so many questions, and now I couldn't think of any of them.

"Even in Antioch you have heard of my son?" she asked with a touch of wonder in her voice.

"Yes, there are many stories, but no one knows what is true and what has been exaggerated."

"I understand."

For a few moments she sat quietly and then changed the subject as she looked down at the birdcage. "I suppose you heard me singing that silly little song. The bird likes the song and joins in enthusiastically. It is the song one sings to a small child. I used to sing it to my son when he was a little boy, and he would clap with happiness."

For a moment we both sat quietly, she with an air of contentment and I with growing frustration as I tried to form a question. Finally I broke the silence.

"I have heard that an angel appeared to you in Nazareth."

"Does that seem strange to you?" Her gaze was steady but puzzled.

"Very strange."

"It seems less strange to me now than it did when he appeared beside the well in our garden. After all that has happened, all the miraculous things that have happened, how could it have been otherwise? The prince of heaven, the Messiah, was coming, so it is not strange that Gabriel himself would make the announcement."

"Gabriel?" I asked.

"Yes. He said he was the angel who stood continually in the presence of God."

"Could you see him?"

"Oh yes." She clasped her hands and spoke with enthusiasm. "It was wonderful. He was strong and powerful, surrounded by a great light. There was a fragrance like flowers in the air and a sound of many harps."

"Were you afraid?"

"Not really afraid, just in awe," she said, speaking slowly and deliberately now. "There was such love—you can't imagine. I felt love, almost unbearable love, for me. I couldn't understand it."

"And . . . ?"

"Then he said my name. He knew me. 'Fear not, Mary,' he said. 'You have found favor with God.'"

"Did he bring some message?"

"Yes, of course. He said I would conceive in my womb a son, and I should call his name Jesus." Her hands flew to her stomach, and she paused before speaking again. "He said many other things that I didn't understand then. I did ask him one question. I was betrothed to a man named Joseph, but I had not been with any man. So I asked him how I could have a son."

"And what did he tell you?" I leaned forward and waited for her answer.

"He said it would be of the Holy Spirit that I would conceive, and the child would be called 'the Son of God.'"

I was stunned into silence. There was no doubt in my mind that she had seen an angel—but that the angel had told her she

 19

was to conceive without a husband, and that the child would be called "the Son of God"? This was very difficult for my analytical Greek mind to comprehend.

"I know you must find this difficult to believe," she said, as if sensing my skepticism. "I understand. I myself found it almost impossible to believe. If it hadn't been for what the angel told me after that, I suppose it would have been even harder."

"What could he possibly have said that made this easier to understand?"

"He told me that my aged cousin Elizabeth, who had never been able to conceive a child, was already six months pregnant. I must have looked astonished, because he added, 'With God nothing shall be impossible.'"

We both sat very still thinking about the strangeness of it all. I could see that this was all as fresh in her mind as though it had happened the day before.

"Then did he leave?" I asked.

"No. He waited for an answer from me."

"What could you possibly say?"

"You must understand; all of us had been praying, pleading, crying out to God to deliver us from the oppression of the Romans. Herod was bent on killing anyone who opposed him—especially those like my family, who were of the house of David. 'O Lord God,' we prayed, 'send your holy Messiah to rescue us.'" She spoke with great animation. "None of us ever thought about how he would come. I suppose we thought he would come like Gabriel had come. But that was not what God had in mind."

Even in Antioch I had heard of the hope for the coming of a messiah. "Do all of your people believe a messiah will come?"

"It has been prophesied since the very beginning." She adjusted her mantle with a strong, sure movement.

"How strange."

"We believe . . ." She hesitated and studied my face as though remembering I was a Greek, ". . . that in the beginning, our God gave a curse and a promise. The curse was because of evil and deception, and the promise was for blessing."

"And this blessing . . ."

"Eve, our first mother, was deceived and had to be punished. At the same time, God gave her a promise that through her seed the deceiver would be crushed. The one who was promised we call the Messiah, the Anointed One, a Savior." She glanced at me with a questioning look as if checking to see if I understood.

"And Gabriel came to tell you that you were to be the mother of this Promised One?"

"He told me I was to bear a son who would be called the 'Son of the Highest.' His name was to be Jesus, which means 'savior.'"

"He gave you a chance to refuse?" I leaned forward, determined to understand.

"Yes. I didn't have to accept. But with tears of joy running down my face, I answered,

'Behold, I am the handmaiden of the Lord. Let it be unto me according to all you have spoken.' And he disappeared from my sight."

"How could you accept so willingly? Did you realize the problems this would cause when you tried to explain to your parents how you had become pregnant?"

"Of course, I had no idea of the problems. I was so excited that at last the Messiah was coming and that I had been chosen and had been found worthy of this trust. I thought everyone would rejoice with me. Our prayers were about to be answered." She smiled, a lovely, wistful smile.

"And then, of course, there were problems."

"Oh yes. My parents explained to me that very few would believe my story. I could be stoned as a harlot. Joseph would find it hard to believe and probably wouldn't marry me. I could see right away that they doubted my story. My mother paced the floor crying, and my father couldn't even look at me but began to moan and clutch his heart as though he were dying. 'I must go tell Joseph this bad news immediately,' he said."

"And Joseph? What did he say?"

She didn't answer right away but worked a fold into the edge of her mantle. "In the end, my father couldn't bring himself to go to Joseph. 'Let's wait,' he said. 'We'll think of something.'"

"Was there no way you could convince them of the truth?"

She took a deep breath and then said, "Finally I remembered what the angel had said about my cousin Elizabeth. She was old and had been barren all her life, but he said she had conceived. I begged them to let me go visit her and see if what the angel had told me was true. My father agreed to take me. 'Whether it is true or not, Mary will be spared the prying eyes of the village,' he said. 'And that way we won't have to tell Joseph right away.'"

"So no one believed you?"

"No one—until I came to the house of my cousin. Gabriel had visited her husband and told him that his wife was going to have a child and that they were to name him John. He was in the temple at the time, officiating at the altar of incense. He didn't believe such a thing was possible, and Gabriel told him he wouldn't speak until the baby was born. We could see that my cousin was pregnant and that her husband couldn't speak."

"Did that convince your father?"

"Yes, but it was still hard for him to believe, and he kept saying that he couldn't understand it." She looked down and pressed a knuckle to her trembling lips. "Of course, he had been with the devout men who had pleaded, begged, and cried out to God to send a deliverer, a messiah, but he had imagined his coming in a very different way. Finally, in utter confusion, he decided that I should stay with my cousin until her child was born. 'She will need help,' he said, and I knew he still

27

couldn't face the people of Nazareth, who would never understand."

"But you did go back to Nazareth?"

"Yes. My father came to get me when the six months of my cousin's confinement were up. The child had been born and named John, just as the angel had instructed."

"Were all the problems solved then?"

"Oh no." She hesitated. "Everything was worse. My father looked at me and saw that I was great with child, and tears of frustration came to his eyes. My cousin tried to talk to him, and her husband made an effort to encourage him, but it was useless. 'We will have to tell Joseph,' he said as he guided me out of the house and headed down the road that led back to Nazareth.

 28

"As soon as we reached home, my mother burst into tears at the sight of me. When my father tried to explain, she became almost hysterical. 'Who will believe such a thing?' she cried. 'We will be the butt of every joke and the laughingstock of the entire village. And if it proves to be of God, can't he see we've suffered enough? How cruel.' Then my mother flung her mantle over her face and wept bitterly." For a moment Mary could not go on.

"My father must have seen that I was experiencing a terrible shock. He led me out into the garden so I would not hear my mother crying. 'It will be all right,' he kept saying nervously." She turned her head away so I would not see her tears.

"He went back into the room to talk to my mother. They must have decided that he should go right away to explain everything to Joseph. This was even more disturbing to me."

"You couldn't trust Joseph's love?" I asked after a brief pause.

"You must understand our customs. I had never even seen Joseph except at a distance, and of course, I had never talked to him. I knew his mother and his sister well, and that was as it should be in Nazareth. He had been picked for me because he was of the same background as my family, the house of King David.

"At the betrothal I was wearing a veil. Until the marriage, no man, not even the groom, was to see me. It was a simple ceremony. Our fathers signed an agreement, and some baked goods were passed with our best grape wine. My father knew the men of the family well and was impressed with Joseph. He was a scholar but practiced carpentry to earn a living. This was a custom of our people. All fathers wanted their sons to be scholars, but life was uncertain and so they wisely had them also learn a trade."

"I can understand why all of this was so difficult for your family," I said. "They had made a good match for you, and now everything would be spoiled. Did your father curse his God for making all this trouble?"

"No." She shook her head so forcefully that her mantle fell back on her shoulders. "That would never have been the way of my father. He simply decided that he must go immediately to tell Joseph."

"And . . . ?"

"My father was gone a long time, and when he returned, we knew the news was bad, very bad. He sank down on a bench inside the door and, pushing back his headpiece, he leaned against the wall and shut his eyes as though he were exhausted. My mother rushed to him and begged him to tell us what had happened. He groaned, and my mother began to weep.

"'Ann, don't weep,' he said. 'The good Lord will help us. Mary has done nothing wrong.'

"I was so touched by my father's confidence that I ran over and threw my arms around him and wept with him." She pressed the end of her mantle to her trembling lips.

"It was not until bedtime that he felt he could tell us what had taken place at the house of my betrothed. 'They were, of course, terribly disturbed,' he said. 'It was too much. They couldn't understand.'

"Finally, Joseph's father, Jacob, had said that his son was a man and could decide the issue himself.

"My father almost choked on the words as he told us what Joseph had said. 'He was very kind,' he said, 'but puzzled.' He assured my father that he would not bring me to public disgrace but, instead, would put me away quietly."

"What did he mean, 'put you away quietly'?" These customs were so foreign to me—I feared the worst.

"Usually, if a woman is found to be pregnant and is unmarried, she is brought to the public square and stoned to death. Joseph was saying that he would not demand such a punishment, but would prefer the whole thing be dealt with as quietly as possible. Of course, he was not going to marry me."

"What did you think of all this? You must have been very upset." I realized my voice had grown husky with emotion.

"There are no words to tell you how frightened I was. By now I was well aware of the seriousness of my condition.

 34

"I went to the roof with my sleeping pad and tried to sleep, but I was too distraught. No one believed my story. They couldn't imagine such a thing. All night long I was remembering everything the angel had said and weeping as I prayed for mercy. I knew the angel had said that with God all things are possible, but I had no faith that he could rescue me and this small child that would soon be born. I wept for myself and for my child."

"And were you rescued?" I asked. I could hardly imagine a good outcome to her story.

She looked at me and smiled. Seeing how disturbed I was, she reached out and touched my hand. "I know now that God does hear us and answers when we cry out to him for help," she said. "I didn't know that then."

"Are you telling me that help actually came?" I asked.

"It came in a way I could not have imagined. Just as the sun came up, there was a loud knocking at our front gate. I ran to the edge of the roof and looked down. There was Joseph and his father and grandfather. They were pounding on the gate. I saw my father go to the gate, and I observed his surprise when he opened the gate and found his three old friends standing there smiling. 'We have good news,' the old grandfather said as he stepped inside the gate.

"That was all I could hear from the roof, and it was only later that my father told me what had happened. When Joseph had gone to bed that night, he'd been greatly disturbed by the decision he'd made. He prayed and slept fitfully until suddenly, just as he dozed off, an angel appeared in a dream and told him that he must not be afraid to take me as his wife. The child I carried was of the Holy Spirit, and his name should be Jesus, meaning 'savior.'"

With that amazing story, my first conversation with Mary, the mother of Jesus, came to an end. She invited me to stay and eat with some of Jesus' friends, but I was too excited about all I had heard. I felt that I must get back to my room and write a letter to Theophilus telling him everything that had happened. John had also agreed to take me along with Mary to visit Bethlehem. "She has wanted to go back and visit the place where Jesus was born," he said. "Every memory of him is very precious to her."

Every day for a week, I went to see if it was time for the trip to Bethlehem. Several times I found Mary working at her loom. "I am weaving a prayer tallith," she said. "It is a shawl every Jewish man must have for his prayer time. It covers his head and his shoulders, closing him in to concentrate on his prayers. I have always woven the clothes for my family, and I enjoy it very much. I once wove a very special seamless robe for my son, but it was taken by the soldiers while he was on the cross. They cast lots for it. John says this was predicted by the prophets."

Another time she was making the challah loaves for the Sabbath. I watched her take down a wooden bowl, place in it some dough left over from the day before, and then add flour and water. She set it aside and watered her plants while she waited for the dough to rise. When it had risen, she began to move and push and fold and press until it was smooth and pliable.

"Why did you put the leftover dough in the bowl?" I asked.

She laughed. "It is fermented and makes the new bread rise. Of course, when we make the matzo bread for Passover, it must have no leaven in it at all. In fact, during the Feast of Unleavened Bread, we get rid of every bit of leavening in the house."

I watched her again separate a part of the bread and asked her why she did this. She looked at me. "You aren't used to any of our customs, are you?" she said.

"No," I admitted, "but I would like to understand."

"There are many sacred things about making bread," she said. "It's a special gift from God. He gives us the seeds for the wheat, and it is his sunshine and rain that make them grow. It is all a divine mystery. When I make the loaves, I am a part of this miracle. So I separate part of the dough to make a loaf to be taken to the priests in the temple as a thank offering."

With that, she went back to preparing the dough in a carefully braided form and left it to rise. When it was finished, she gently placed the bread on woven trays and gave them to the serving girl to take to the ovens to be baked.

All this time I had been studying the scroll containing her genealogy. I had become interested in her genealogy when John told me that it was very much like Joseph's. They had both descended from Israel's great King David, and that is why their lives had been in jeopardy, forcing them to leave Jerusalem and move to Nazareth. Herod had believed that if he could destroy all the descendants of King David, he would feel secure on the throne.

"What is the difference between your list of ancestors and your husband's?" I asked.

Her hands were still covered with flour as she came over and looked at the scroll I had unrolled. "You will notice," she said, "that David had two sons that are especially featured in the genealogies. One is Solomon and the other is Nathan. My genealogy comes down through one of David's sons and Joseph's through the other."

It was getting late and I had many things to attend to. And I could see she was too busy to talk. I excused myself and walked with Mary to the front gate. There was something I wanted to ask her—a favor—but I felt it was presumptuous. I hesitated, and when she noticed, she asked, "Is there some problem?"

"No, not a problem," I said.

"Then you wish to ask something?"

"That is true. I wish to ask a favor, something that would mean a great deal to me."

"Don't be afraid to ask. I can always say no." She had such a gentle, understanding way about her that I suddenly felt free.

"We Greeks," I said, "are not satisfied to live without being able to express ourselves in some artistic way. It is not enough to have a profession such as medicine; we must also be making music, writing poetry, or painting. I am a painter. Usually, if I am going on a trip, I take along my art supplies and paint whatever interests me. I didn't intend to bring them with me this time, but I found, to my surprise, that my friend Theophilus had put them in secretly. He also wrote a note asking me to paint a picture of you. He put it this way: 'If you find the stories to be true, I would be interested in a picture of this woman. Surely she is a most unusual person. Without a picture, I may doubt she even exists.'"

She laughed. It was only the second time I had heard her laugh. "How strange," she said, "that this is so important to your friend."

She had no idea that people were interested in her. She had known she was important to her son, but she could not imagine being important to people who didn't even know her.

"Would you mind," I asked, "if I made a sketch some day, right here in your courtyard? I can do the actual painting in my room."

She hesitated, then agreed, and the next day the sketch was made.

A few days later I had completed the painting. When I told her it was finished, she begged to see it. "I have never even heard of such a thing," she said.

It was true. Since the making of graven images was forbidden by Jewish law, she could not imagine a painting, let alone a painting with herself as the subject.

The next day I brought the painting for her to see. It was done in dark colors on a piece of olive wood. It was a fair likeness, but I had painted her as being serious. I had not captured the pleasant, cheerful side of her nature.

She studied it a long time before she spoke. "I suppose," she said, "since you made it, you could just as easily have made me young."

"Of course I could have made you young, but I felt that for Theophilus it would be better to portray you as you are. Is there any reason you wanted me to paint you as young?"

"Oh yes," she said. "I would have liked my child to be in the picture also. After all, he is the one who is important."

"I don't paint children very well," I said hesitantly.

"But I can see you're very talented. I'm sure you can do anything with your brushes, and you can easily fix this by just adding the baby." She was pointing to the right side of the picture and smiling with such excitement that I couldn't refuse her. It would be a very poor likeness, but I wanted to please her more than anything.

With just a few words of agreement, I picked up the picture, wrapped it in my cloak, and hurried out the door. I knew it would look strange for an older woman, as I had portrayed her, to be holding a baby, but since she saw nothing wrong with it, I decided to do my best.

It was almost another Sabbath before I finished the picture. I don't paint children well, as I had told her, and this attempt was no exception. The child was not at all attractive. However, on the first day of the week, I carried it over for her to see.

"There," she said, "now it's perfect." She didn't seem to notice anything wrong. It was simply another miracle to her.

As we waited for John to make the final arrangements for us to visit Bethlehem, I talked to many people who had known Jesus. They told of miracles and parables, of his concern for sick people and his insistence on time alone for prayer. As I listened to them, I began to wonder what he thought his mission was. Why had he come at this time and to this place? I decided to ask his mother. Surely she had heard him express his thoughts on the subject.

I waited until the general work of the morning was finished, and then I asked her the question. "Who did Jesus say that he was? Did he ever say why he had come?"

She stopped and looked at me with that piercing awareness that gave the impression I had asked a question she found important. She sat down near the grape arbor and motioned for me to sit on the bench opposite her. She didn't say anything right away but fingered a loose prong on her egg basket.

She seemed intent on working it back into place and was not in a hurry to answer my question. By this time I had learned to wait patiently for answers. I found that she had pondered all these questions and had her own answers that must be stated just right.

She looked up and studied my face as if to see if I was ready for her answer. She must have been encouraged, because she set the egg basket on the ground beside her, clasped her hands on her lap, and began to explain.

"Most people were disappointed," she said. "They thought the Messiah would solve all our physical and political problems. They had talked about it for years and were convinced they knew exactly what the Messiah's coming would mean to all of us. But that wasn't at all what he had in mind. 'My kingdom is not of this world,' he said, and we all puzzled over that. Then he said things like, 'I came that you might have life and have it more abundantly.' Most of us could only think of having a better life by having more riches, but that isn't what he meant."

"Did you ever find out what he did mean?" I asked.

"I suppose we're still finding out," she said, adjusting her mantle.

"But the kingdom he was talking about, what did he mean?"

"He did say at one time, 'The kingdom of God is within you.'"

"How very strange. Did anyone understand what he was talking about?"

"In the end we could only watch what he did and determine what he meant by his actions."

"Is there anyone who understood what he meant?"

"There are many who have caught a brief glimpse, and they are the ones who followed him, watching everything he did and listening carefully to what he said."

"It must have been wonderful to have been healed by him. I would like to sit and talk to Lazarus. To be raised from the dead—what an extraordinary experience!"

"Lazarus has gone to Cyprus," she said. "He felt it might be a place where he could go to spread the good news about Jesus. However, his sister is here, and she had an interesting experience with my son. It was at a time when she was rebellious and out of control. She had gone to Capernaum, and there she became involved in a very irreligious and even sinful way of life; but she was miserable. Perhaps she will tell you the rest of her story."

"How can I find her? Her story may help me understand who Jesus was."

"If you wait here, you will see her. This is the day she usually comes down from Bethany to bring me eggs."

As it turned out, I had only a short time to wait. There was a soft knock on the outer door, and within minutes the two women, Mary the mother of Jesus and Mary from Bethany, were greeting each other. I had only this brief time to study the visitor. She was slight and delicate, wearing layers of filmy garments that swirled and eddied gracefully around her. The mantle had fallen from her head down around her shoulders, revealing a veritable cascade of curly brown hair. She brushed it back from her eyes with one hand and set the basket she carried down on a ledge. I could see the basket was full of white eggs.

Mary said something, and I noticed that the visitor looked around the courtyard until she spotted me. She smiled, and Mary brought her over to where I was sitting under the grape arbor. "This is Mary, the sister of Lazarus I told you about. She says Lazarus has gone to Cyprus, but she will be glad to answer any questions you may have. She doesn't have much time today, but she comes often, so you may see her again before you leave."

With that, Mary motioned to a stone stool, and the visitor sat down and adjusted her skirts before looking up and smiling at me. "What do you want to know?" she asked.

"I did want to know about your brother Lazarus, but now that my hostess has told me of an interesting encounter you had with the Rabbi, Jesus, I would like to hear your story."

She blushed and looked down, nervously fingering the folds in her dress. "It is a difficult story for me to tell," she said in a low voice. "I am so ashamed. You must understand—I had been very foolish. I was a great embarrassment to my family." Here she paused, and I noticed a tear rolling down her cheek. She brushed it away with her hand and glanced at me to see if I still wanted to hear her story.

"You don't have to give any details. I am mainly interested in how you met Jesus and what he said to you."

Her expression changed, and she looked relieved. She paused for a moment as if remembering the incident and then began speaking slowly, sometimes closing her eyes as though actually seeing Jesus sitting at the table in the house of the Pharisee. "That Pharisee was so rude," she said bursting out with such feeling that I was surprised. "He had asked Jesus to dinner and then didn't even carry out the basic niceties. He had many servants, but he never asked a one of them to wash the Rabbi's feet.

"I'm an impulsive person. When I saw that kind, loving man being so mistreated, I couldn't stand it. I had just been to the apothecary and had bought an expensive alabaster cruse of rare perfume. I rushed into the house, past the doorman, and over to the table. Before anyone could stop me, I had uncorked the jar and poured some of the ointment on Jesus' feet. I didn't have a towel, so I used the only thing I had—my hair. As I remember it, I wept and dried his feet while the Pharisee said terrible things about me. He told Jesus I was an evil woman and scoffed at him for letting me wash his feet.

"Jesus rebuked the Pharisee, reminding him that no one had washed his feet when he entered and that I had both washed his feet with the ointment and tears and wiped them with my hair. Then Jesus did an astonishing thing—he turned to the men who were ready to throw me out and said, 'Her sins, which are many, are forgiven for she loved much.' He told me my sins were forgiven and that my faith had saved me. Then very gently he said, 'Go in peace.' He didn't embarrass me by telling what my sins were, nor did he condemn me as the scribes and the Pharisees would have done.

"From that moment on I have loved him as I have never loved anyone else," she said. "He gave me hope and changed my life." With that, she burst into tears, and I decided that this was not the time to ask her about her brother, Lazarus.

The trip to Bethlehem soon became a reality. Donkeys were borrowed, provisions were organized, and the relatives in Bethlehem were notified. There was to be no sleeping in the stables on this trip. Mary, of course, wanted to visit the stable where she and Joseph had found shelter the night when Jesus was born, but she didn't want to linger in its cold, damp darkness. The rains were about to descend on Bethlehem along with the cold. It would be necessary for those who were going to have warm clothes and a comfortable, dry place to sleep.

It was taken for granted that I was to go with them. Though I told no one, I had a secret desire to find one of the shepherds who had been out on the hillside that night tending his sheep. I didn't think this would be a difficult task, since there were many in Bethlehem. I was fascinated by the appearance of angels that kept edging into this story. No one else seemed to realize how strange it was that at every turn these people made, an angel appeared to guide them.

I had gotten the family name of some men who were shepherds. It became evident that this was an occupation inherited by certain families. If the father was a shepherd, then the son would also become a shepherd. It was a hard, tiring job with very little reward. They were practical, silent men who would never imagine anything. If they said they saw an angel, then one could be sure they had seen one.

The day before we left, Mary came and motioned for me to follow her. She led me to a backroom where some of the family belongings were stored. I immediately spotted a small carved chest sitting on a pile of sheep skins. It was clumsily made, with lilies carved into its surface. "He is the lily of the valley" was carved around the outside, while on the inside was the word "beloved" in crude Hebrew script.

"This box is supposed to have belonged to King David when he was a boy," Mary said. "They say it was carved for him by an old shepherd. As you can see, it is rough and simple. Perhaps that is why no one claimed it and now it is mine. I keep my most prized belongings in it."

She lifted the lid, and I could see only a fold of white linen and some dark objects. They didn't seem to be the kind of thing that would be considered prized or special. I wondered why she treasured such things.

"See," she said as she gently lifted the linen piece out of the box. "This is the swaddling cloth I wrapped him in, and these are the cords that held the cloth in place." Her eyes sparkled with unshed tears, and I could see that this was indeed a great treasure. I wanted to reach out and touch the cloth but was so overcome by her reverence for it that I drew back instead.

As she folded the cloth and placed it back in the box, I again noticed the dark objects. They looked like straps with small leather boxes attached to them. They seemed very plain and out of place. I couldn't imagine why they would be in this box. She must have sensed my puzzlement. "These are the tefillin, or phylacteries, he used for prayer," she said, unfolding the dark objects. "He observed all the laws and customs of our people. In fact, he said, 'I came not to destroy the law but to fulfill it.'"

"I have seen the men here using these when they pray. Does that mean he prayed only in the most formal way?" I asked.

"No, there were many times he went off into the mountains and talked to God, whom he called his 'heavenly Father.'" She gently folded the objects and put them back in the box. "He lived very simply and had few possessions."

"But he did work with your husband in his carpentry shop," I said.

"Yes, he made yokes for oxen and frames for windows. Sometimes, when I walk out in the country around Nazareth, I will see oxen plowing, and I wait at the end of the furrow to examine the yoke. I can always tell if he made it. He worked hard to make the yoke fit the animals' shoulders so the burden they carried was as light as possible. I was always astonished that he cared so much for people and even animals that he would go to extra trouble to make things easier for them."

I watched her put the box back on a shelf and then turn to leave. "Tomorrow morning early," she said, "we will leave for Bethlehem. I hope you will not be disappointed."

"And," I said, "what do you hope to find in Bethlehem?"

This obviously caught her off guard. She turned around and gave me a long, penetrating look. I could see she had not even dared to ask this of herself. She looked away, and I saw that she was not ready to answer that question. She simply reached out and lightly touched my hand and then hurried out to greet the guests who were continually arriving.

I stood where she had left me and thought about the strangeness of this trip back to Bethlehem. John had told me that after Jesus was born Mary had never returned. She had never even mentioned wanting to go back, and yet now, suddenly, it was something she felt she had to do. I tried to imagine what would induce her to make this journey, and I thought perhaps she wanted to see if the city had changed much in these last years. Even as I entertained the thought, I knew that could not be the reason. There was some other very important reason. It was a long distance to ride on a donkey, and the weather was getting cold and the rains could start any day now.

I didn't look forward to the journey itself. The Romans were in charge of every road and the many checkpoints, and they were likely to stop us several times and make us unload the animals and wait for their inspectors to come and examine all our belongings. I knew the Romans had strengthened their guard. They suspected little boys and often women of harboring weapons. Even a small caravan advancing toward Bethlehem would not go unnoticed. Every Jew was searched, and when any problem arose, it was a Jew who was brought in for questioning. What the Romans would think of a Greek traveling with Jews, I could not imagine.

We started early in the morning, before dawn. The cobblestone streets of the old city were empty, with only a few shopkeepers arranging their wares. Roosters crowed in far-off courtyards, and the hooves of our donkeys clicked rhythmically on the worn stones. Up ahead an old woman looked down at us from a lighted window and cursed the commotion so early in the morning.

When we came to the Joppa Gate, the Roman soldier refused to let us pass. "These gates remain closed from sundown till sunup. You should know that," he growled. There was no alternative but to wait in the gatehouse for daybreak.

The road to Bethlehem wound around through a valley where the famous King David had fought many battles with the Philistines. It was called the Valley of Rephaim, or the valley of the giants. From there the road descended to a glen filled with roses still in bloom. We left the glen on a broad path and came to a well where we stopped for a drink of clear, cold water. John explained that the Magi were supposed to have stopped at this well on their way to Bethlehem after seeing King Herod in Jerusalem. The Magi had become uncertain as to where the star was; it seemed to have disappeared while they were in the city. It was only as they bent over this well to get a drink that they saw the star mirrored in the water.

There was only one more important place to stop before coming to Bethlehem. It was the grave of someone called Rachel. She had died a long time ago, but her story was so sad it made everyone pause and say a prayer or pass the tomb in silent meditation. John raised his hand, motioning for us to stop. I saw that Mary had already dismounted and was weeping. Both of her hands were on the rough stones of the tomb, her head bent down between them in overwhelming grief. I moved up next to John and asked him what was happening.

"This is the tomb of our ancestor Jacob's wife Rachel. She was pregnant with a child she desperately wanted. She only had to make it to Bethlehem and there would have been help, but here, within sight of the village, the child was born and Rachel died. She named the child 'child of my sorrow.' Mary was very moved by this story. When she came this way with Joseph and passed by this tomb, she was terribly afraid that the same thing would happen to her. She was already in great pain. She begged Joseph to let her stop. Her pains were intense, and the jolting of the donkey was unbearable. 'If I die here it is no matter; the child will live,' she said. 'That is all that matters.'

"'No,' Joseph said, 'you shall not die. We have just a little way further. Our God has chosen you to be the child's mother, and you will not die.' He insisted they go on. Even when they reached the village and could find no room, Joseph remained strong and encouraged her. The stable where they finally stopped was dark and bare, but Joseph made it seem a suitable place for the child to be born. He sent for a midwife and returned to Mary's side as soon as the child was born."

"And now?" I whispered. "Why is she weeping now?"

"Certainly it is out of pity for Rachel and out of gratitude that she didn't die like Rachel on the road to Bethlehem."

Mary let John help her back onto the donkey, and our small procession moved on toward the village. As I passed the rough stones piled so neatly over Rachel's tomb, I also prayed a prayer of thanksgiving that Mary had been allowed to reach Bethlehem and have her baby.

We made one more short stop before we entered the village. It was beside another well not far from the northern gates. It was obviously a well where the shepherds came to water their flocks. I could see the shepherds' fields below in a great bowl-shaped valley. As we approached we saw an old man sitting on the curb of the well. He had the traditional shepherd's crook in his hand, but he was obviously too old to go out after the sheep. He evidently still wanted to see them being brought in for the night.

I sat down beside him and edged up on the subject I was so interested in. "Do you belong to the Ben Ezra family?" I asked.

He slowly and painfully turned around and looked at me. His sharp, suspicious eyes were almost hidden by his shaggy eyebrows, and his tousled hair jutted out from under a worn headpiece. His gnarled hands shook as they clutched the crook. "What do you want of the Ben Ezra family?" he asked.

"I was told they have been shepherds here for generations. If I could find one of them, they might be able to tell me about a strange thing that happened one night a long time ago."

"What kind of thing are you talking about?" he asked. His eyes narrowed, and his whole demeanor became guarded.

"I was told there were angels that appeared over the field, and the shepherds even left their flocks to go into Bethlehem to find the baby they spoke about. Do you know anything about this?" I asked.

"Why are you asking? Who wants to know?" he asked.

"The mother of that baby has come back to visit the stable where he was born. It would mean a great deal to her if she could talk to one of the shepherds who were out tending the sheep that night."

"Where is she?"

"She is the woman standing beside the well, talking to the young man."

I noticed that he turned and looked at her, and for a moment I thought I saw an expression of wonder and amazement cross his face. I was almost sure he knew what I was talking about. But when he turned and looked at me, there was the same guarded look I had noticed at first.

"No," he said. "I don't know about that. I never heard angels or saw angels." With that

he got to his feet and, leaning heavily on his crook, went down the road toward the village gate.

Of course, I was disappointed. I had hoped that he would be able to lead me to some of the shepherds who had been out on the hillside and heard the angels. He was the right age to have been there himself. I couldn't understand why he would deny something so simple.

I didn't have time to ponder the strangeness of the old man's demeanor, for just at that moment a detachment of Roman soldiers came marching down the road toward the village. The centurion shouted an order, and they came to an abrupt halt in front of the well. "Who is in charge here?" the centurion demanded.

"We are on our way to visit our relatives here in Bethlehem," John said, stepping forward.

The centurion walked around, poking at the coverings on the donkeys and making the women untie the bundles they carried. When the vegetables spilled out on the ground, he kicked them contemptuously. Then, jabbing his sword into a basket of fruit, he ordered one of his men to take the basket. "They have nothing of interest. Let them pass," he said.

With that, John helped Mary onto the donkey, and they hurried down the road, passing through the village gates just as they were being closed for the night. Unlike years before when Mary and Joseph had come for the census, the streets were almost empty, and their relatives were waiting for them with roasted lamb wrapped in mint along with melons and a pomegranate drink. They assured us that there was room for all of us for the night.

The next morning John took Mary and me to see the cave where Jesus had been born. It was a cave under a house that often served as an inn when Bethlehem was crowded with visitors. The cave was used for the family's animals and had some sheep that the shepherds hadn't yet taken out to pasture. I watched Mary and wondered what she was thinking. She walked around and touched the cool, dark walls. She ran her hand over the manger filled with hay. Suddenly she turned to me with a puzzled look. "Where were the angels when I was suffering so on the long trip down here?" she said. "And couldn't one of them have managed to find something better for my poor baby's bed? This is what I have wondered so often,"

It was so unlike Mary to complain that we were all surprised. However, having made the short trip from Jerusalem and then seeing the stable, we were appalled at the difficulties she had faced. She had traveled all the way from Nazareth in the north, and it had been the cold and rainy time of the year. Where were the angels? we all wondered.

As we stood in the stable door, a young boy dashed around the corner of the house and came toward us. "It's time for me to take the sheep out to pasture," he said almost breath-lessly. "I'm really quite late, but my grandfather insisted on coming with me. He wants to talk to the lady."

Just as he said that, I saw an old man come hobbling along. He was the same old man who had been sitting by the well the day before. It was obvious that he was trying to hurry. "It's important," he gasped. "I must see her; I have to tell her."

Mary stepped forward, took his elbow, and led him to a bale of hay where he could sit down. "Now," she said, "what do you have to tell me?"

"I was here on that night. I saw you and the baby. It was just as the angels said it would be," the old man gasped.

"You saw angels?" I exclaimed. "What did they say?" I couldn't contain my excitement.

"We were so afraid," he continued. "The light . . . and then the bright, shining angel suddenly appearing in the light. It frightened all of us."

"But what did the angel say?" I urged impatiently.

"The angel must have seen how afraid we were, because he quickly said, 'Fear not,' several times. Then when we stopped hiding our faces and peering at him through our fingers, he said, 'I bring you good tidings of great joy.' I guess we thought he was going to tell us how worthless, evil, and even wicked we were. Instead, he said he was bringing us great joy. Can you imagine that? We were just poor, ignorant shepherds, and he took the time to come and tell us that."

"Is that all he said?"

"No. Then he told us that a child had been born who was to be our Savior and that he was for all people. He had been born that night right in our village, and we would be welcome to go see him. He wasn't in one of the big, fancy houses but in a stable, wrapped in swaddling clothes and lying in a manger."

"And how did it end?" I asked.

"Oh, it was wonderful. Suddenly there was with the angel a great host of angels, praising God and saying, 'Glory to God in the highest and on earth, peace, goodwill to men.' I can tell you we took off right away for the village. Left the sheep for the angels to take care of," he chuckled. "We didn't lose a one of them. We were so excited that I'm not sure we ever did tell the lady here all that had happened and how we knew about her baby."

"You didn't tell all of this to the mother and her husband?"

"Well, you have to understand. Seeing that the angel was right and there really was a baby in swaddling clothes in a manger, we just fell to our knees in awe and wonder. I don't know what we said."

"Why didn't you tell us all of this when I saw you at the well yesterday?"

"I was too frightened. I didn't know who you were, and even when I saw the lady I didn't recognize her."

Mary came over to the old shepherd and gently touched his arm. "Thank you so much for coming and telling me all of this. That night I was so busy with the new baby, and you were so shocked at actually finding us here, that I never really did understand about the angels' appearance." With that, she asked him to tell his story over and over again, and I could tell that his message answered some of her questions.

After the old shepherd left, Mary sat down on one of the bales of straw and looked around at each of us. "Well. That's where the angels were that night. They must have known I was too busy with a new baby to really hear and remember their message. How wonderful that they entrusted the message to the shepherds. Shepherds never forget anything."

"And," said John, "if you had been in a palace or an inn rather than in the stable, the shepherds would not have been able to come to see that there really was a baby in a manger."

Mary sat pondering all that had happened. She had been deeply moved by the old shepherd's story. "The angels are always saying, 'Don't be afraid,' and yet we are so often afraid," she said.

John had noticed something else of importance. "They are also always reminding us that they want to bring us joy—great joy. How sad that we have so much difficulty remembering such things when we are in some dark valley."

For myself, I could hardly wait to return to Jerusalem, where I could retire to the room they had given me and write to Theophilus about all of this. It was a good ending to my first visit to Jerusalem and Bethlehem. In a few days I would be returning to Antioch. And perhaps someday I would come back to visit my many friends in Palestine.

A Word
from the Author

Some years ago when I was living in the Middle East, I had a memorable experience in Jerusalem. My friend, who worked with the United Nations and lived in Jerusalem, offered to take me to her favorite site.

"I am sure," she said, "you have never been there, since most people don't even know it exists." Of course, I was curious and eager to go with her. She was delighted. We started off at a quick pace over narrow cobblestone streets, up dark allies, around crumbling walls and locked gates. She stopped to let me catch up. "This is the al-Mujahideen Road," she said. "It leads straight to the Lion's, or St. Stephen's, Gate."

I now knew where I was. St. Stephen's Gate is where tradition says St. Stephen was stoned to death, and it is also the gate through which Israeli soldiers broke into the city during the Six Day War. I assumed this was the place she wanted me to see.

"No, no," she said, laughing as she motioned me off to the left and through another gate. There, suddenly before us, was an amazing sight. A cathedral of stark simplicity, but with a strange beauty, rose up from a platform of gray stone.

"Those solid, skyward-thrusting walls have more than a hint of Norman, Crusader strength," I exclaimed.

"You're right," she said. "It is a Crusader cathedral and happens to be one of the best examples of Norman work."

"What is it called?" I asked, thinking it must be named for one of the disciples.

"Saint Ann's Church," she said and waited to enjoy my surprise.

"But who was Saint Ann to have such a splendid memorial built in her honor?" I asked.

"Saint Ann was Mary's mother and the grandmother of Jesus. This marks the place where the house of Mary's parents stood. Down through the years there were churches built here, but they were all destroyed. Then, when the Crusaders came, they wanted to build a cathedral on this spot so it would be remembered."

"How strange," I said. "I always pictured Jesus and his family living in Nazareth."

"So have most people," she said.

I loved the cathedral and treasured the story behind its existence. I learned, as I studied the accounts of Jesus' birth and the history of those times, that the house of Saint Ann was right beside the pool of Bethesda and very close to the Jewish temple area. This suggests that, being of the lineage of King David, they were involved in affairs of the temple. This could place them in a position to pose a threat to King Herod, who ruled from 37 B.C. to A.D. 4. During this time he conscripted thousands of Jews to work on the new temple he was building. He was fiendishly cruel and killed not only people in his own family but anyone who threatened his authority. It is recorded that he hunted down descendants of King David with the same vigor that he killed the five thousand babies in Bethlehem, just to make sure no descendant of David would rise up and lay claim to the throne. What could be more logical than for the Jews, who would have been threatened in this way, to move quietly to Nazareth? That would have involved quite a few families and probably would have included Joseph's family.

When Herod died, the immediate threat no longer existed. Though the new ruler was cruel, he did not feel as threatened by the descendants of King David. For this reason, I have assumed Mary would have moved back into the old family home. This means that as the story opens Mary is receiving Luke in the house that was on the site that is now St. Ann's Church.

Luke was a Greek physician from Antioch (Col. 4:14). There is considerable evidence that he was originally from Macedonia and went to medical school in Philippi. As a Greek and a Gentile, he brings a unique perspective to the story. He has nothing to prove. He is not a Jew and knows nothing about the coming of a messiah. Undoubtedly, he would ask different questions and would examine miracles with more knowledge.

I have made use of the first few verses in the book of Luke, where he gives his motive for investigating the stories about Jesus—the fact that there are so many stories that no one knows what to believe. For those who have longed for a credible, eyewitness account of the events surrounding the life of Jesus and his followers, Luke does very well. The Greeks were known for their analytical approach to life, and as a physician he had a good grasp of reality.

Because of his detailed account of Christ's birth, Luke seems to have gone directly to Mary as the one person who would really know the truth about Jesus. He obviously listened very closely as she told about angels and the messages they brought. He had come looking for truth, not with the intent of inventing a good story.

I have included no fact or story that is not in Luke's Gospel. For this reason, the story of Lazarus's resurrection from the grave is not included. However, the story of his sister Mary is, even though I had to go to the book of John to get all of the facts. Luke tells us of a woman who came into the house of a Pharisee, where Jesus was having dinner, and anointed his feet with her tears and a precious ointment then wiped them with her hair. In John 11:2 we are told that Mary, the sister of Lazarus, is the woman who anointed Jesus' feet in the house of the Pharisee. I included this story because it shows Jesus' attitude toward sinners and gives us insight into the family in Bethany that he loved.

It is a fact that tradition also describes Luke as an artist, and there are several paintings in existence that he is supposed to have painted of Mary. We will not be surprised by this if we realize that the Greeks were very artistic people. It would not be strange for a Greek to have a profession as a physician and at the same time be a painter. These paintings are in the Vatican today.

I have been enthusiastic about this book because it is Mary who really knew who Jesus was. She had seen and heard the angel's announcement and had become pregnant, as she says, "without knowing a man." Of course she expected miracles and blessings and undoubtedly could not understand why he didn't free them from Roman domination. Other people saw and doubted because their expectations were not met, but Mary couldn't doubt, and so she pondered.

Many people have contributed to the success of this venture, and it would not be right not to name them.

First, I must give great credit to my agent, Olga Weiser, who is also a Greek and could give some good advice; my beloved editor, Lonnie Hull DuPont; and Sheila Ingram and Kelley Sytsma, who had to jump in at one point to keep the ball rolling. Of course, I have to mention my youngest son, James, who nudged me into learning to use the computer. Then there are my two sons on the island of Cyprus, Philip and John, who have given valuable advice. There is my daughter Debby Carrick, who is a valued resource person, and her daughter Sharon, a student at Wheaton, who did a very good pre-editing job. Then there is Paul, who didn't read the manuscript or even touch it but pulled many practical irons out of the fire so I could keep on writing.

It is impossible to name my many friends who have been a constant encouragement, but I would be remiss not to name a few: Sylvia Lacey, Linda Underwood, Jeanne Ridley, July Moon, Mary Lynn Anderson, Margery Bensey, Susan Phipps, Nancy Miller, Ruth Githens, and Mary McKinnon, all members of the Knoxville Writer's Group. There have been others: Leona Choy, a well-known writer herself; Pat Brigance, an able research enthusiast; and Debby Way, an expert in advertising and selling books.

Roberta Kells Dorr is known for bringing some of the Bible's best-loved people to life through her biblical fiction. She has written many novels, including the best-selling *David and Bathsheba*. She lives in Maryville, Tennessee.